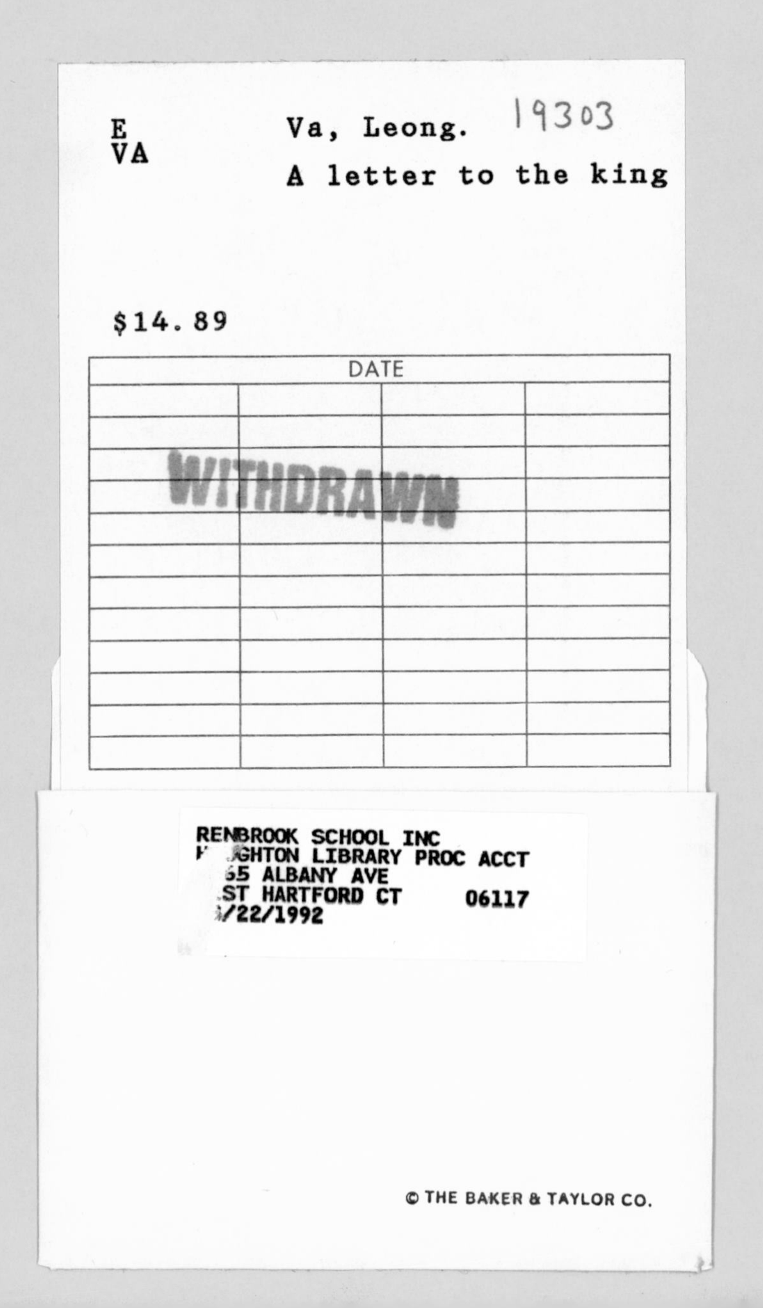

A LETTER
TO THE KING

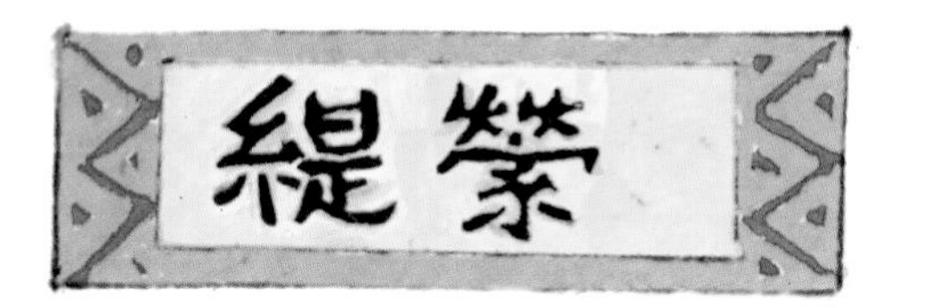

Story and pictures by Leong Vá

Translated from the Norwegian by James Anderson

長城

THE GREAT WALL
OF CHINA

漢初•孝文十三年•齊•

Once upon a time in China, more than two thousand years ago, there was a small village right next to the famous Great Wall. In those days parents wanted only sons, because they thought sons would be able to look after them better when they grew old.

生草藥

MAKING HERBAL
MEDICINE

太倉令淳于公無男•有五女•

In the village there lived a doctor. Like everyone else he wanted a son, but had only daughters. Five of them. The youngest was called Ti Ying. Each day she and her sisters helped their father with his work.

A NOBLEMAN

公有罪當刑，徒繫長安。將行，

One day when a relative of the king's was visiting the village with his son, the boy was taken ill. The doctor was sent for, but it was too late; there was nothing he could do to save the boy's life. When the king heard about this, he ordered the doctor to be brought to the capital and thrown into prison.

考服

MOURNING CLOTHES

The king's men came to the village to take the doctor prisoner. When the time came to say good-bye, all his daughters stood weeping.

"If I had a son, he would have done something to help me," their father said angrily. "My daughters only know how to weep."

椿磨

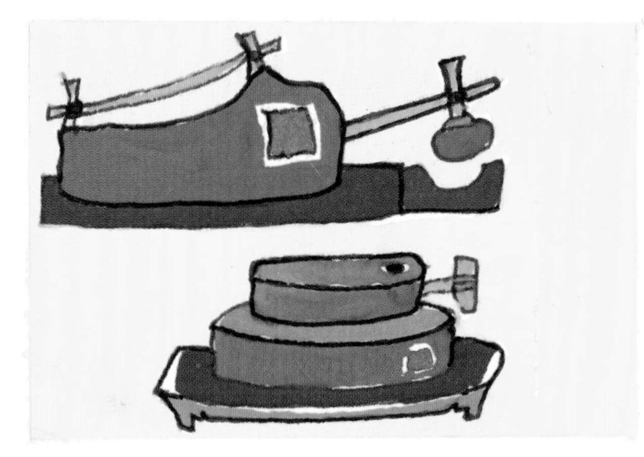

A RICE MILL

少女緹縈，與其赤尾駒相泣。

Little Ti Ying had a small horse by the name of Red Tail to whom she always turned when she was unhappy. Now she decided that together they would go to the capital with her father. Perhaps there was something she could do to help him.

鯉魚枷

A PILLORY

The journey to the capital was long. They walked and walked, through forests and across plains and bridges. Ti Ying let her father ride Red Tail when he was tired. They passed a woman by the roadside selling tea, but Ti Ying did not notice her; she thought only of how she could help her father.

盆栽

A BONSAI

至京•修書•欲呈天子•

When they got to the city, Ti Ying's father was thrown into prison.
Ti Ying wrote a letter to the king. She hoped the palace guards would help her get her letter to him. In those days there was neither post office nor mailman, and ordinary people never saw or met the king. He lived in The Forbidden City surrounded by many guards.

紫禁城

THE FORBIDDEN CITY

Outside The Forbidden City Ti Ying met two huge palace guards, but they paid no attention to her because she was a girl. Since the king came out only when he went to the temple to pray, Ti Ying hoped the priests at the temple would help her.

A PRIEST WITH A MASK

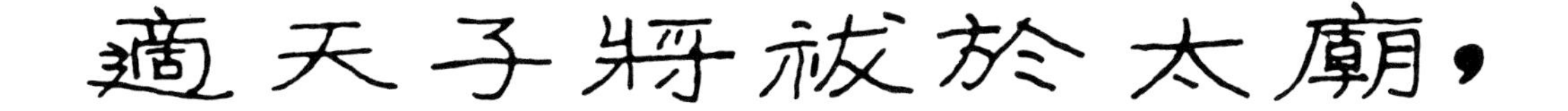

Ti Ying hurried to the temple. But the priests were so busy practicing the "mask-dance," which they were to dance for the king, that they did not even notice Ti Ying. It was then that Ti Ying decided to give the letter to the king herself.

御車

THE KING'S CARRIAGE

On the day the king set out for the temple, Ti Ying and Red Tail hid behind a tree and waited for him to come. Guards walked in front of the king's carriage making sure no one got too close to him. Anyone who dared disturb the king would be severely punished.

漢文帝

THE KING

上至，縈疾出，冒死上書，

As the king and his train drew near, the guards in front shouted, "Make way, make way for the king!" Just then Ti Ying sent Red Tail out into the middle of the road, making the king's carriage come to a stop. The guards shouted, "Who dares stop the king?" While they were trying to catch Red Tail, Ti Ying ran up to the king with her letter.

MANDARINS
(public officials)

曰：『妾自願沒入官奴，以贖父罪』。

The king was very surprised that a girl had stopped his train. He read the letter, which said, "Dear King, My father is the only doctor in our village. He has saved many lives, and if he is put in prison, many sick people will suffer. So I beg you to set him free, and let me go to prison and serve his sentence for him."

獄

A PRISON

上憐悲其意，免其父刑。

The king was so moved by this girl who cared so much for her father and the people in her village that he gave orders that the doctor should be set free and allowed to return home with his daughter.

Ti Ying was overjoyed and ran to the prison. Her father cried with happiness as he embraced his daughter.

什技者

ACROBATS

淳于公之得超生•賴其女也•

There was a great feast and much rejoicing when they returned to their village. Ti Ying wore a lovely dress the king had given her. She danced with her sisters, and everyone in the village was happy.

Now they no longer believed only boys could look after their parents. Especially Ti Ying's father, who was glad he had five daughters.

A LETTER TO THE KING

First published by Det Norske Samlaget, Oslo, Norway

Typography by Elynn Cohen
1 2 3 4 5 6 7 8 9 10
First American Edition, 1991

Library of Congress Cataloging-in-Publication Data
Vá, Leong.
[Brevet til kongen. English]
A letter to the king / story and pictures by Leong Vá ; translated from Norwegian by James Anderson.
p. cm.
Translation of: Brevet til kongen.
Summary: When Ti Ying's father is put in prison, Ti Ying, his youngest daughter, is able to save him by writing and delivering a letter to the king.
ISBN 0-06-020079-0. — ISBN 0-06-020070-7 (lib. bdg.)
[1. China—Fiction.] I. Title.
PZ7.V12Le 1991 91-9469
[E]—dc20 CIP
AC